Jack Schaefer has been called "the most convincing tale-teller now writing fiction about the period of Western expansion," and in Old Ramon he has created one of his most magnificent characters. Beautifully written and filled with wisdom as well as adventure, this story of an old shepherd, a small boy and two brave dogs, has a trueness and depth that make it timeless and ageless in its appeal.

Ramon has been put in charge of his patron's boy for a season with the sheep. As his father and grandfather had before him, the boy watches and learns from Old Ramon: about sheep, rattlesnakes, sandstorms, coyotes, and wolves; how to overcome fear, ease tension, face death and responsibility; the difference between being alone and being lonely — all valuable things that can be learned not from books but only from such a man — a man with "the feel of the flock born in him."

For Old Ramon is as much a part of the plains as a gnarled juniper, a man who is wise in the ways of sheep, and the ways of men and of boys who are becoming men. He will make a lasting impression on readers of this book.

Old Ramon

by Jack Schaefer

illustrated by Harold West

Houghton Mifflin Company Boston

The Riverside Press

Number

1385593

Old Ramon

1   THERE IS no other animal so stupid as the sheep," said Old Ramon. "No other. Not one."

"There is the chicken," said the boy.

"The chicken?" said Old Ramon. "Yes. The chicken is stupid also. But he is no animal. He is a bird."

"The birds belong to the animal kingdom," said the boy.

"And who put such foolishness in your young head?"

"It says that in a book at my school."

"In a book." Old Ramon hunched back farther into the thin shade of the stunted juniper behind him. He looked down at his work-knobbed hands. He examined the cracked nails of his blunt old fingers. "Then it must be so. But such book-talk means nothing to a man of my years. It is for you that you study the books. And when you are a man, and a grandfather, you will not speak words that a boy can make wrong."

From high overhead in the clean blue of the sky the sun of early summer sent its golden light over the big land, searching out the shadows everywhere, filtering through the meager branches of the junipers. Old Ramon sat still, head low, and studied his work-knobbed hands, and the boy looked at him, at the big old head under its ancient cone-crowned wide-brimmed hat tied with a string beneath the chin, at the broad flat face with deep-sunk eyes looking downwards now and cheekbones strong under shrunken old skin and big nose bent sideways by some blow of the far-gone past and wide flat mouth notched askew at one corner by the scar of a long-ago knife cut.

"You are my book about the sheep," said the boy.

Old Ramon picked slowly at grains of sand under a cracked nail. "And how is that? I am only an old man who cannot even read in a book."

"You are a man who takes care of the sheep for my father as not one of the others can do. You lose no lambs. You bring in your flock fat and well fleeced. My father says it has been so since he was a boy and you took care of his father's sheep."

Old Ramon's head rose. "My patrón says that?"

"He says it. He said to me: 'You will go with Ramon for this season. You have had too much of the printed books. You will watch Ramon and learn. If he will talk to you, you will learn more.' "

Old Ramon looked off into sun-shimmered distance, toward the far greening foothills of the mountains. Silent, seeming motionless, the flock rested nearby in small bunches crowded into the thin shade of other junipers. Silent, motionless except for panting tongues, the two dogs lay in another patch of shade. Silent, motionless except for occasional switchings of its tail, the burro drowsed under its lashed packs close by another juniper.

"I am listening," said the boy. "My ears are open."

Old Ramon looked at the boy. The hard lines of his old face of a pirate, of a bandit, softened a little. "There is no other animal except, it must be, for the chicken that is so stupid as the sheep." He leaned back, against the low branches, and his eyes closed as if he searched inward for the words. "As the sheep. Not the flock. The flock is stupid also but not in the same way. The sheep, one sheep, is like the finger of a man that has been cut off. The finger then is a nothing. But as a part of the man it is a something. It is a part of the something that is the man. And so with the sheep. One sheep is a nothing except as a part of the something that is the flock. . . . Always it is that you must hold the flock in your mind. Not this one sheep and that one sheep but the flock. . . . I cannot explain this to you as could a man who writes a book. But it is so. . . . One sheep does not think. He does this or he does that and there is no sense to it. But the flock thinks. And what the flock thinks each and every one sheep in the flock knows at once and all together. It is strange but it is so. . . ."

Slow moments moved and Old Ramon sat quiet, against the branches, and the boy sat quiet, cross-legged, in neighboring thin shade, and Old Ramon pushed out from the stunted juniper and rose to his feet. "Do you see? The flock is stirring. Not this one sheep or that one sheep. The flock. At once and all together. The flock knows that the hottest hour of the day has passed. The flock thinks now of moving, of finding food. Do you not see how it is itself shaping itself? . . . That is Theresa in the front and others follow her. She was with me last season and she is with me now because she is one that others follow. . . . That is Juanita to the side and others follow her. That is Maria to the other side and she has those who follow. But all in the same direction. In the direction of the flock. . . . It is only the part of one day that we have been out with these sheep and already they have shaped the flock. Each one sheep knows now his place. And always now it will be like this. The same ones will be in the front. The same last ones will be the last ones. And that is good. It is that now, if they act otherwise, we will know there is a wrongness somewhere we must find and make right."

Old Ramon picked up his worn stick and leaned on it to watch the slow drifting movement of the flock. The boy stood beside him. The soft muted blethering of the sheep came to them, the ewes calling to their three-month lambs, the lambs blatting gently in the seeming sheer joy of life and movement, all of it the social humming of the flock. In their patch of shade the two dogs lay still but their heads were raised. The young black dog watched the moving sheep. The old brown dog watched Old Ramon.

"I do not understand," said the boy. "How is it that you know that is Juanita?"

Old Ramon straightened a little in surprise. "Because it is Juanita and no other."

"But they are all the same. Each one is like the others. The young ones that are still lambs and just starting their wool, they are smaller and move about more. But the old ones, they are all the same."

"The same?" said Old Ramon. "But they are

6

as different as — as the people. No. The people have more differences but the sheep have their differences also. I have not thought of this before but it is so. It is that a good pastor knows each and every sheep in his flock when he has been with them for some days and his dog knows also. I am not certain because I have not thought about this before but I think it is not any one thing about the one sheep. It is the allness of that sheep. It is the shape of him, the way he is fleshed, the way he moves, the way the wool grows, the setting of the ears, the hang of the tail, the looking about, the cropping of the browse. Not any one of these things but the allness of them. Ramon will know each and every one of these sheep in a few days. It is new to you. But by the time that we reach the hills, you will know many of this flock."

— Old Ramon leaned on his stick and the boy stood beside him and together they watched the flock. The young black dog rose and trotted over by the boy and nuzzled against him. The old brown dog lay still in the patch of shade, head up, and watched Old Ramon.

"Do you see? The flock thinks that the graze will grow better to the south where the ground falls away to the Arroyo Hondo. And the flock thinks right. But that is private range. We are journeying to the hills where there is also good graze, and free graze, and for many weeks. We must go west. But not true west. Not even Ramon and his Pedro can make a flock journey into the eye of the sun. We will go southwest until the sun hides behind the mountains and then we will turn toward the Ojo Frio by the red rocks for water and the night."

Old Ramon looked toward the brown dog and nodded his head. The brown dog rose and trotted after the flock and the black dog saw the other moving and leaped forward, eager and anxious, and followed and bounded ahead and came back and followed and bounded ahead and came back and followed. Close behind the flock the brown dog stopped and looked back. Old Ramon raised his left arm outstretched shoulder high and swung it forward in a wide sweep, a wide gesture southwestward. The brown dog trotted ahead and to the left of the flock and swung in by the leaders and nudged against shoulders and nipped at flanks and pressed them toward the right and the black dog followed and bounded and barked and nipped.

Old Ramon leaned on his stick. "Gently, gently," he murmured. "Ai, that Sancho. Will he not watch Pedro and learn? . . . Now . . . That is enough." Old Ramon put two fingers in his mouth and whistled. The brown dog stopped and looked back. Old Ramon raised his right arm straight above his head and dropped it down pointing as the flock now drifted. The brown dog trotted forward and around the front of the flock to the right side and the black dog bounded after. The brown dog turned and snapped and the black dog, abashed, retreated again to the left side and the flock drifted slowly southwestward between the two dogs.

Old Ramon motioned to the boy to take the lead rope of the burro. "Now we follow. Now the flock thinks that the direction we want it to go is the direction it has wanted to go. But it goes slowly. That is right because it must feed on what there is along the way. But it goes too slowly. For four days, perhaps it will be five, we must follow behind and push. Gently. Always gently.

A flock must not be driven, must not be made to go fast, except in time of need. It is not like a herd of the horses or of the cows. To go fast unsettles the sheep so that they do not feed well even when the graze is good and they lose flesh. But a flock can be gently pushed and made to think that it wants what we desire that it wants. We will follow behind and push until we have passed the Jornada Seca, the dry place that is the journeying of a long day and into the night and where there is little graze and no water. After that we will go in the front. The flock will know that we are coming near to good pasture and will begin to hurry. Perhaps it will smell the good grass up in the hills. Perhaps it will be that Theresa and Juanita and Maria will remember from last season and what they know the flock will know at once and all together. But too much hurrying and there is not enough feeding along the way. We will go in the front and hold them from the hurrying. . . ."

2   O<small>LD</small> R<small>AMON</small> sat on his blanket that
lay flat on the ground near the embers of the little
fire. He leaned against the red rock that loomed
behind him big and black in the dim starlit darkness. The old brown dog lay by his feet, a dark
shape on the ground, with its muzzle stretched
out on its forepaws toward the flock that lay
bedded in a wide clotted grayish patch on the

bush-dotted level beyond. Thirty feet away the spring trickled from the rock outcropping of the slope behind to meander down to the small pool where the flock had watered. The boy squatted by the spring and scrubbed four tin plates and two tin cups with handfuls of sand and rinsed them in the trickling water. The young black dog crouched beside him and watched every move.

The boy took the plates and the cups over by the fire and laid them on the ground. The black dog followed, close by his heels.

"I think," said the boy, "that perhaps I am almost as good a washer of the dishes as someone else here is a preparer of the food."

"There is the pan," said Old Ramon. "And the coffeepot."

The boy looked at him and quickly looked away and hurried to take the pan and the coffeepot from the other side of the fire and go to the spring again and the black dog followed, close by his heels.

The boy came again by the fire and set the pan and the pot on the ground by the plates and the cups.

"The place for such things is in their bag," said Old Ramon.

The boy straightened and looked at him. "And why is that? We will have need for them in the morning."

"Always one must put all things in their places," said Old Ramon. "Then if there comes a need to move quickly, all is ready."

The boy looked down and scuffed at the ground with one foot. Slowly he bent and gathered the things and went over by the packs on the ground near the picketed burro and stowed them in a faded empty flour sack. He took his blanket and came back by the fire and spread this on the ground. He sat on the blanket, cross-legged, and the black dog lay beside him and pushed its head into his lap.

"Yes," said Old Ramon. "Yes. That has shaped itself also."

"The dishes?" said the boy.

"No," said Old Ramon. "Nothing of the dishes. It is of the dog. Yesterday that Sancho was my dog. He is by my cousin Romero's Hugo out of Fidel Hernante's Nicole. He came to me from that

Fidel who has owed me the price of three sheep since the winter of the big snow when life was hard and there was little meat. Fidel brought him to me. 'I have forgotten the sheep,' I said to him. 'And I have my Pedro.' 'I have not forgotten,' he said to me. 'I have no sheep and no money. I have only many children. But my Nicole she also has the children and here is one of them.' What is a man to do when another man wishes to pay a debt for the easing of his own mind? . . . Ai, yesterday that Sancho was my dog. Even this morning he was my dog. And now this night he is your dog."

"My dog?" said the boy.

"Of a certainty. He has decided that."

"Do you mean my dog to keep?"

Old Ramon thumped a hand down on the blanket beside him. "Of a certainty. Ramon does not speak just to make words. What a good dog decides, a wise man accepts. . . ."

 ̄ The embers of the fire faded and winked out one by one and the boy scratched the black dog's head in his lap and gently pulled one of its ears. Old Ramon stirred on his blanket. "Pedro."

The brown dog raised its head and turned it to look at him. "Pedro. It is time. Go to the flock." The brown dog rose and trotted off into the darkness. Old Ramon looked at the boy.

"Can he not stay here with me?" said the boy.

"His place is with the flock."

Slowly the boy stood up. "Go, Sancho. Go to the flock." The black dog started away and turned back and licked the boy's hand.

Old Ramon thumped a fist on the blanket beside him. "You must make him go!"

The boy stepped back from the black dog. He stamped one foot on the ground. "Sancho! Go to the flock!" The black dog started away and stopped and looked back and whined softly and trotted off into the darkness.

Old Ramon slid himself down until he was stretched full length along his blanket. He pulled one edge over him and then the other. The boy stared into the darkness after the black dog. Slowly he lay down on his blanket and pulled the edges over him.

The boy shifted on the ground and wriggled inside his blanket. The voice of Old Ramon was muffled as it came from within his wrapping. "Ai, the ground is hard. But it is that it becomes more soft each night. . . ."

The boy had scrouged small hollows for his hips in the loose sand beneath his blanket. He lay still. The voice of Old Ramon came again. "I do not yet know if he will be a good sheep dog. But I think it is that already he is a good boy-dog. . . ."

3   THE FLOCK drifted forward in the warmth of midmorning sun. It browsed in slow shifting seeming uncertain movement as small bunches lagged and then spurted to overtake the others. Out on the two sides trotted the two dogs and stopped to sit on haunches with tongues panting and trotted forward again. And behind walked Old Ramon swinging his stick in rhythm with his

long slow strides and beside him walked the boy leading the burro.

"I think," said the boy, "that the tending of the sheep means a muchness of walking in the sun."

"It means that," said Old Ramon. "Always it is so on a journeying. But when we are in the hills there will be the shade of the bigger trees and the days of sitting still. Of Ramon sitting still and watching the sheep put on good flesh and grow good wool and thinking of the many years of his living. And I think that he will be watching a boy play boy-games with a dog. . . ."

The flock drifted forward and the ground sloped away in far gradual descent to a vague curving line of reddish willow brush-clumps and a few big cottonwoods.

"And now we must cross that little river," said Old Ramon. "And we must have care. There is nothing that shows the stupidness of the sheep and of the flock like the water. I have known a flock that went almost mad with the thirst because it would not drink from a pool, the one pool for many miles around, and good water, that a strange flock had visited and left there its smell. And yet at another pool that another strange flock had visited it might drink with no noticing. I have heard of flocks that lost many dead sheep because they broke away and could not be stopped and ran to water that everyone knows is bad. And when one must cross the water — ai, then there is no knowing. Perhaps the flock will cross as if it is a nothing, a little splashing in the water and that is all. Perhaps it will refuse and turn back and make the trouble. There is a good crossing here, not wide but good, where the water is not too fast and not too deep. But there is no knowing. . . ."

Old Ramon stopped and leaned on his stick. "It is time. Now call your dog to you."

The boy put two fingers in his mouth and whistled and the black dog leaped around and came bounding to him.

"Good," said Old Ramon. "But you must teach him about the whistling. One time is to look, to see what is wanted. Two is to come. . . . Now fasten the burro to that bush and wait here. You will see how Ramon and his Pedro have care at a crossing."

Old Ramon strode forward, swinging his stick

to match long strides, and as he strode he put two fingers in his mouth and whistled and the brown dog stopped and looked back. Old Ramon swung his right arm out in a sweeping gesture around and back to his chest and the brown dog raced forward and in front of the flock, between it and the low sloping near edge of the little river that was about fifty feet away, and stopped the leaders and raced back and forth holding the flock there as the stragglers moved up crowding in from behind. Old Ramon strode to the front of the flock and with his stick reached and pushed and prodded and cut out forward six sheep and herded these toward the water. The rest of the flock was bunched in close order now, intent, those in front standing motionless, legs braced against jostling from behind, staring, watching. The brown dog swung away from them, leaving them standing braced and staring in their silly stupidity, and raced to help Old Ramon, and the six sheep were at the water's edge, sniffing at the shallow swift current that roiled noisily over small rocks and pebbles. They pulled back from it and tried to turn away.

"Ai," said Old Ramon. "They would be stubborn today." One of the sheep at the water's edge broke away and the old dog, a streak of dark brown against the pink-flushed tan of the ground, headed it and brought it back and the rest of the flock stood and stared and watched. Gently, gently, but firmly, Old Ramon and the brown dog pressed and prodded and compelled the six sheep to face toward the water again. Suddenly Old Ramon raised his right hand and pointed at one of the sheep, at Juanita, and the brown dog lunged forward and leaped upon her hindquarters and his weight pushed her into the water. She stumbled and caught her footing and moved ahead and Old Ramon pointed again and another was in the water and the others surged forward, following.

Old Ramon strode into the water that swirled about his legs to the knees and urged the sheep forward and Juanita pulled herself dripping out on the other low sloping bank and moved on, seeming to forget in the instant the water just past and still dripping from her, already dropping her head in search of forage, and the others followed.

Old Ramon strode back to the near bank and

already the brown dog was racing to the rest of the flock, swinging in at the side of those in front to start them moving. There was little need for urging. The flock saw the six on the opposite bank and wanted to be with them and moved forward, the first stepping into the water as if it were a nothing and the others following. And Old Ramon on the one side and the brown dog on the other side pressed them inwards, funneling them down to the crossing.

Back up the sloping the boy stood and watched and the black dog crouched quivering and eager by his feet. "We must stay here," said the boy. "That is what we were told." He stood straight and looked out at the flock, the three hundred sheep flowing forward in a wide stream that narrowed down to the crossing, and at an old man and old brown dog working together, silent and intent, in the swift sureness of knowledge and the years.

There were stragglers at the rear of the flock, the late ones, the slow movers, the always behind. The boy saw Old Ramon wave at him to bring them forward.

"It is our turn, Sancho," said the boy and ran toward the stragglers, and the black dog, eager and anxious, bounded ahead and nipped at flanks and the stragglers jumped, startled, and hurried after the flock.

— But the black dog, too eager, too anxious, too excited, began barking wildly and nipping harder and the stragglers broke into the bunched rear of the rest of the flock that had not yet crossed the river and these, startled in turn, began to scatter and run to the sides along the bank and some pressed forward in desperation and crowded those in the water and there was floundering and frantic scramblings on the uncertain footing of the river bottom.

"Ai!" shouted Old Ramon. Blood rushed into his scarred bandit face. Anger shook his voice. "That fool! Hold him!"

The boy ran, calling, grabbing, and caught hold of the black dog and crouched with his fists tight in the thick fur of the dog's neck. He looked up and saw Old Ramon hurrying, hurrying, leaping on tireless old legs and with reaching stick, and the old dog a brown streak here and there and everywhere, the two of them heading, turning, gathering the scattered sheep and herding them to the crossing.

"Name of God!" cried Old Ramon. Two sheep had been crowded and jostled down in the river and carried by their own floundering and by the current downstream into a pool. There, silent in the way of the sheep in danger, they struggled in the water, their heads bobbing up as their fore-feet flailed under the surface, but with the weight of the water soaking into their fleeces pulling them down.

Old Ramon dropped his stick and threw off his hat and ran to the pool. With long strides he strode into it. The water rose to his waist, to his shoulders. He had one of the sheep and thrust it through the water ahead of him to the opposite bank and as he heaved from behind it pulled itself out. He turned back for the other. Only its nose showed and this too was sinking. He came to it and ducked down out of sight in the water and straightened with his right shoulder under the sheep and heaved and struggled toward the bank. He worked along the bank to its lowest point with the sheep hanging limp over his shoulder and

24

heaved it out on the dry ground and crawled out
after it. Still on his knees he turned the sheep so
that its head lay down the slope. Its eyes were
closed and water trickled from its mouth. He
worked over it with big knobbed knowing hands.
More water trickled from its mouth and its eyes
opened and its head thrashed feebly and its legs
began to kick in little jerks and suddenly it scrambled to its feet and staggered some sideways and
moved away.

Old Ramon rose to his feet. His breath came
in great gasps. Water dripped from all of him and
muddied the ground around his heavy old boots.
He looked toward the flock. It grazed along the
gradual ascent from the river to the level beyond
and it was shaped into a flock again and the two
sheep from the pool were joining it and in front of
it an old brown dog stood guard, holding it there,
waiting. Old Ramon moved his head to the side.
Fifteen feet away the boy stood, straight and still.
His legs were wet from the river. In one hand
he held the lead rope of the burro and in the other
Old Ramon's hat and stick. At his feet crouched
the black dog, cringing some and ashamed.

"Ai!" said Old Ramon between gasps. "I was

the fool — to bring that fool!"

"We are sorry," said the boy. He stood a little straighter. "But he is like me. He has to learn."

"To learn!" said Old Ramon. "It must be born — in the dog — as in the man!"

The boy looked down at the ground by his feet. His shoulders sagged a bit and he seemed to shrink smaller. He scuffed at the ground with one foot and did not look up. "I will take him back," he said. "I will carry food and follow the way we came. We are only nuisances that get in the way of your work."

Old Ramon stood still, very still except for the movement of his chest seeking breath. He turned his head and looked on down the little river where it flowed into the distances of the big land and was lost around the curve of a far low ridge. The last drops dripped from him and the warm sun dried those on his face and still he stood looking into the distances of the big land. "Ai," he said softly. "I am old. I forget what it is to be young."

Old Ramon strode over by the boy. He took his hat and plopped it at a jaunty angle on his head. He took his stick and thumped it on the ground and leaned on it. "We will have no more foolish talk about nuisances. What is a little splashing in the water? It is a bathing. There are those who say that never does a sheepman have a bathing, an all-over washing, except when a sheep falls into the water and he must pull it out. I think it is that now Ramon has had a good bathing." He turned toward the flock and put two fingers in his mouth and whistled, once, twice, and the brown dog started around the flock and trotted toward him. He turned again to the boy and pointed with his stick at an angle up the long low sloping from the river. "Do you see that mesa rising there to the southwest?"

"I see it," said the boy.

"That is the way we are going. Straight toward it and then around it to the left."

The brown dog had come close now and sat back on its haunches and looked up at Old Ramon.

"Pedro," said Old Ramon, pointing at the boy. "That one will be your master for a time. You will do as he directs."

The boy stood straighter, staring at Old Ramon. "But — but I do not understand."

Old Ramon reached to take the lead rope from

the boy's hand. "I think that the way to learn is to do. You will take the flock as I told you. You and my Pedro and your Sancho. You will start the flock in the right direction and push it, gently, gently. I will sit here and pour from my boots the water I feel around my toes and perhaps I will rest for a moment. And then I will follow."

The boy stood straight and still. He saw that the brown dog looked now at him. He saw Old Ramon holding the stick out toward him. He took the stick. He was not tall enough to lean with his hands on the rounded knob at the top but he took hold lower down and leaned on it. He looked at the brown dog and nodded his head and the brown dog trotted away toward the flock, and the black dog, seeing the other move, bounded after but did not bound ahead and stayed behind and followed. The boy too started away, swinging the stick in rhythm with slow strides.

Old Ramon wrapped the lead rope of the burro around one wrist and sat down on the slope of the riverbank and tugged at one old boot. "Ai," he said softly. "I am the fool. I forget. . . ."

4   The sun was low in the western sky, tipping the purpled peaks of the mountains. Its slant light flowed and skipped over the big land, blessing the long rolling rises with golden benediction, leaving hollows of luminous pink shadow between. The last of the flock watered at a small pool in the lee of a low cliff. Old Ramon leaned on his stick and watched them. He stepped for-

ward to hurry them off to join the rest of the flock a short distance away. He strode back near the pool where the boy had unfastened the packs and picketed the burro and was starting a small fire.

"They will graze some now," said Old Ramon. "And soon they will bed down. They will not stray far. Pedro will hold them." He looked down at the boy's bent back. "And your Sancho."

The boy looked up at him quickly, gratefully. "Sancho has been good today. But we have been hurrying since early in the afternoon. Why is that?"

"It has been to reach this watering place in time," said Old Ramon. "I have work to do while still there is light." He strode over by the packs and took one of the ropes that had lashed them. He came back by the fire. "Have you not noticed something different along the way today?"

"That we have been hurrying. That is all."

"Have you not noticed Maria? How she has twitched and bitten at her own flank? How she has rubbed herself against the bushes? How she has tried to scratch herself on the rocks?"

Old Ramon strode away toward the flock. In a few moments he came back leading Maria by

30

the rope tied around her neck. Suddenly he bent low and swept his arms around her legs and pulled them from under her and she fell with a grunt on her side. Quickly he flipped the rope in and out around her legs and pulled it to hold them tight together. She struggled some and then lay still, eyes staring, silent in the way of the sheep.

Old Ramon strode again over by the packs and hunted through one of them, the one that had not before been opened and that contained the little tent and some of his secret things and carried strapped to it his old single-shot rifle. He came again by the fire and he carried a short-stemmed old pipe and a small bag of tobacco and a short piece of hollow reed. "I told myself," he said, "that I would not begin on the tobacco until we were in the hills. The pipe is a friend by the fire in the evening. But always I am too greedy and the tobacco is gone before the season in the hills is finished. I told myself to wait. But we have need of it now."

Carefully he filled the pipe and took a small stick burning at one end from the little fire and held this to the bowl and drew in until the smoke came in good puffs. He tossed the stick in the

31

fire and with the pipe in his mouth knelt by Maria. Deftly, surely, his work-knobbed old fingers began to search through the short tight-curled wool along her flank.

"Ai," said Old Ramon. "Come here and you too will see."

The boy went to him and knelt to put his head down close by Old Ramon's head and peer into the wool. There, in the tiny hollow where Old Ramon's fingers held the wool apart, on the skin, he saw the small dark somehow repulsive spot that was no spot because it moved sluggishly on many tiny legs to crawl out of sight.

"Yes," said Old Ramon. "The tick. The sheep tick. That is a young one. There will be an old one here somewhere that has made many of these young ones. We must get rid of them before they spread to the other sheep."

While the boy sat back and watched, Old Ramon moved the pipe into one corner of his mouth and tucked the small hollow reed into the other corner of his mouth. He drew in deeply on the pipe and with his fingers opened a small place in the wool and bent lower and blew the smoke through the reed into the hollowed place. Quickly he closed the wool over the spot and held his hand spread over it. He waited a moment and opened another place about an inch away and drew in deeply again and bent again to blow the smoke into this spot and closed the wool over it. He raised his head and spoke between teeth clenched on the pipe and the reed. "There is that in the smoke of the tobacco which kills the tick. But I will be puffing and blowing like this through most of her wool. Perhaps you will see how you can do as the preparer of the food. . . ."

The sun dropped below the mountains and flaming color streamed up the western sky behind them and caught itself in reflection of fire on the few clouds floating serene against the deepening purpling blue above and the dusk of the evening slid over the big land. Old Ramon knelt by Maria, sending the smoke of his pipe searching through the tangled curls of her wool. The boy was busy about the fire.

Old Ramon released the rope from Maria and stood up. She lay still a moment and suddenly scrambled to her feet and ran toward the flock. Old Ramon strode after. In a while in the deepening dusk he came back where the fire made its

33

small brave circle of light and the two dogs followed him. "The flock is bedded," he said. "It is content now after the hurrying. And now it is that we are hungry. Ramon and his Pedro and your Sancho." He went to the packs and put his pipe and the tobacco and the reed away. He took the gun and slipped a shell into the breech and leaned the gun against one of the packs where it would be ready in any case of need. He came back by the fire.

The boy was scooping a stew made of beans and dried meat and more beans onto the four tin plates. He looked up. "I am not proud of myself. I think that I have used too much chili."

"Too much chili?" said Old Ramon. "There is never too much of the chili. It is one of the gifts of the good God to his children. It burns out the sicknesses. It makes the strong thirst in this land that makes a man need much water. And it cleans the dust out of the throat as no thing else can. We will have no more talk of too much chili. . . ."

Slow moments moved and the two dogs licked off their plates and trotted to the pool and the sound of their lapping was clear in the stillness of the first hush of the night and they came back and lay down, the brown dog by Old Ramon, the black dog by the boy. Old Ramon and the boy sat by the fire eating in the silence of good appetites. Old Ramon cleaned off his plate and set it down beside him and drained his third cup of black coffee and set the cup down on the plate. The boy finished too and set his plate down beside him and his cup on it. Old Ramon reached to his own cup and rattled it a little on the plate and looked at the boy. 1385593

The boy looked straight back at him in the firelight. "I prepared the food."

Old Ramon thumped a hand on the ground. "And I took care of the ticks." He pushed up to his feet. "There is one way to decide such a thing. We will toss the coin." He searched in a pocket of his shapeless old trousers that had been patched until there was little of the original cloth left and had patches on the patches. He pulled out a small round piece of metal that shone in the firelight from the constant rubbing against the cloth of the pocket.

"I will take the heads," said Old Ramon. He flipped the coin spinning in the air and caught it in his right hand and slapped it down on his left wrist. He peered at it. "Ah, it is the heads. Do you see?" He held the wrist toward the boy, and the boy too peered at the coin.

Slowly the boy rose and began to gather the dishes. He was turning toward the pool that had settled now clear and clean in the dim darkness when Old Ramon spoke, softly, with a small chuckle in his voice. "Mother of God. I cannot do it. To one who thinks himself so clever like my cousin Pablo, yes. To the son of my patrón, no. Look you now at this and see." He held out the coin and turned it over slowly between his fingers. Both of the sides were the same.

Old Ramon tucked the coin back in his pocket and took the things from the boy. "There was not too much chili," he said. "But there was enough. There was enough even for Ramon. When we are in the hills I will show you how the sheepherder makes his bread. There is a trick to it, to bake it through, on the top as on the bottom, with no oven, in the pan, on the open fire." He moved away toward the pool.

5 THE LAND stretched away dry and barren, seeming level but broken by shallow rough sandy arroyos, spotted here and there by stubborn groupings of the low creosote bush that can survive the dryness even of the desert. Off in the distances an occasional dust devil whirled up briefly and died away. The flock rested, endured rather, the shadeless pressure of the midday sun,

standing in small bunches with heads dropped under each other's bellies out of the open glare. The burro stood motionless with dangling lead rope, eyes closed, patient in the lesson of the life of its kind, that to wait out all things and to endure is to live. And Old Ramon and the boy and the two dogs crouched in the meager shade of a blanket laid over four sticks stuck in the ground.

The boy licked his dry lips. He seemed to shiver a little even in the hot stillness under the blanket. "I did not know that the sun could be like this. I think that it frightens me."

Old Ramon looked at the boy. He saw that the boy's eyes were open wider than usual, that they stared more at him with a kind of a glaze over them. He thumped one hand on the sandy ground. "Like this? It is a nothing. This one day only and into the night, and we will be in the cool of the shadow of the hills. It is when there is day after day and no change and only the sun of the desert and there is no water that the men and the sheep know what it is to be close to the madness. I have known it. I was with the father of your father when he took a flock, and a big flock, west to the California."

The boy's eyes no longer stared. Interest had him. The heat that pressed about his body no longer held his mind. "Tell me," he said.

"I will tell you," said Old Ramon. "Ah, he was much man, the father of your father. He was not rough and thick like Ramon. He was slender and he stood very straight and what Ramon could not do with the strength he could do with the cunning of the mind. He was young and I was young, and we thought that together there was nothing we could not do. There were the two of us, and we had three dogs. We paid with a few sheep to the Indians through whose lands we passed, and all went well for many weeks, and we crossed the river that is called the Colorado, and we were very proud of ourselves. And then we came to the desert that is called the Mojave. We talked as we could in signs with some Indians we met there and they drew a map for us in the sand to show the watering places and we went on. We had to push the flock hard because it was long to go. Two days of dry march and we reached the first of the watering places and it was low but there was enough. Two days more and we reached the next watering place and it was low, very low, barely enough. We spoke of turning back but we did not. Ai, we were young and brave and very foolish. We went on. At the next watering place, and that was three days, there was only a little moisture showing and we had to dig and hold back the sheep and wait for the water to seep into the holes, slowly, very slowly. We spoke again of turning back. But to go back was as far as to go on. We went on. And at the next place, two days more, there was no water. Even the digging was useless. What could we do? We went on. I do not know how many days. The water that we carried with us was gone and the sheep were dying along the way. We walked like men who wander in their sleep and one of the dogs disappeared and another died and we did not even stop to bury it. On the last day that was the last because we could not have gone longer we saw far ahead by low hills some greening that meant water. It was many miles, many more than it seemed. We forgot the sheep. We forgot everything but the water. We staggered and we stumbled and we fell often and he held me up and I held him up and I think — I am not certain because it is difficult to remember out of that madness — but I think that at the last I had him on my back and I crawled on my hands and my knees like the beasts. And we reached the water, that was a small stream a man could step across, that came out of the hills and died in the sands. God be praised that we were not so mad to drink fast and bring on the cramps that can kill. . . . When we were ourselves again we thought of the sheep. We thought to go back and save what we could. But there was no need. The flock was there, close to us, what remained of it, and crowding along the small stream. The dog, the one dog that was left, had brought it to the water."

Old Ramon thumped a hand on the ground. "Ah, that one was a dog of dogs. He was the father of the father of the father of my Pedro."

At the mention of his name the old brown dog lying by Old Ramon's outstretched legs raised its head and turned it to look at him. "Eh, Pedro," said Old Ramon. "You know, do you not? It is the blood of his blood that is in you."

The boy looked at the brown dog and quickly looked away and at the young black dog lying by his own outstretched legs and reached to stroke him. "And then?" he said.

"And then we went on. We went toward the mining camps in the valleys of the high mountains, of the Sierra Nevada, where there was much gold but little meat. The sheep were thin and poor but they brought much money. They were the sheep of your grandfather and I was to be paid only for the helping. But when he had the money he divided it in two parts and made me take the one of them. Ai, he was much man, the father of your father. With his part of the money when he was home again he bought sheep, many sheep. And when he died in a fall from a horse he was a true patrón with many pastores working for him. . . ."

Old Ramon took off his big cone-crowned old hat with one hand and with the other wiped around his head where the hot band had pressed. He put the hat back on at a new angle. "Ai, my mouth it is dry from the talking." He took the canteen that hung by his side on a thin strap over one shoulder and pulled it around into his lap and unscrewed the little cap that was like a small cup. The boy watched him and took his own canteen and did the same.

"Two mouthfuls," said Old Ramon. "That is

enough at the one drinking. To drink often but only a small bit at the one time is the way to make the water last and do the most good. And you should hold each mouthful in your mouth for a time before you swallow it." Twice he raised his canteen to his mouth and twice the boy raised his. Then Old Ramon held the cap of his upside down in one hand, making it into the small cup, and carefully poured water into it. "Pedro." He held out the cup in his hand and the old brown dog reached with its head and carefully lapped the water. The tongue flicked gently, gently, and took the water and did not spill a drop.

The boy watched, fascinated. He took the cap of his canteen and carefully filled it. "Sancho." He held out the cap-cup and the young black dog lapped at the water and in his eagerness spilled some and poked his nose against the hand and spilled more. The boy flushed and turned his head. Old Ramon was apparently intent on recapping his canteen and adjusting it at his side. Quickly the boy poured more water into his cap-cup and held it out for the black dog.

"The drinking too is a trick," said Old Ramon.

"It too has to be learned. And we have enough of the water. There is only this one day of the desert. . . ."

Slow moments moved and the heat pressed down over the big land. But the eyes of the boy did not stare with a glaze over them. He sat still and he was thinking of the grandfather he had never known except in a stiff old crayon portrait and of Old Ramon whose bandit face had looked down on him in his cradle and many times since and of the two of them together in the desert called the Mojave to which this little desert was nothing and of the two of them young and brave and foolish. . . .

"What was it," said the boy, "that you did with your part of the money?"

Old Ramon looked off into the heat-shimmered distances. "I did what Ramon has always done with the money when it has jingled and burned in his pocket. I spent it . . . on much wine . . . and, yes, on the women . . . and at the gambling table. . . ."

Abruptly Old Ramon pushed up and out from under the blanket and pulled it from the upright sticks and began to fold it. "We cannot wait for the flock to think to move. The stupid sheep will stand for hours in this sun. Pedro! Make them to start to move! We must push them steadily the rest of this day. . . ."

Harold E West

6   THE FLOCK plodded steadily under
the slant relentless glare of the afternoon sun. It
moved as a flock, almost as a single sprawled shifting thing flowing slowly over the land. There
was little movement within it. Only a few sheep
hesitated briefly to nibble at the tiny dark waxy
leaves of the few creosote bushes and to investi-
gate the ground close under these bushes in whose

meager protection a few small stunted tufts of hardy grass might have taken root. Nothing seemed to move in the whole of the big land except the flock and the two dogs out on the sides and Old Ramon and the boy and the burro plodding steadily behind. There was no real sound from the sheep, no soft blethering of the flock, only occasional coughing or blowing in the dust and the rustle of many small split hoofs in the sandy soil.

A shudder of new movement ran through the flock. Those in front were stopping and others were moving up by them and they were forming a circle around a small space. They faced inwards, staring inwards, with their heads stretched out some, and a strange shrill blatting came from them.

The boy licked his dry lips. "What is that?"

"It is the snake," said Old Ramon. "They say the rattlesnake. There is nothing else that makes them blather in that way. And the stupid ones will not go around it. They would stand like that and make their silly noise all the day. Follow and stay behind me and you will see."

Old Ramon strode forward into the flock, pushing his way through the sheep. The boy dropped the lead rope and followed. They reached the

47

center circle of open space and the boy saw, out in the middle, the snake with thick body coiled and small flat head raised and the tail tipping out of the coils and whirring the rattles that could not be heard through the shrill blatting of the sheep.

Old Ramon motioned to the boy to stay back and he himself started forward, his knobbed stick ready in his hands. But the black dog had come bounding in after the boy and now rushed past him, past Old Ramon, barking furiously, and darted toward the snake. Old Ramon leaped and swung his stick with the strength of both shoulders behind it and knocked the dog sideways and away and it yelped and retreated back by the boy and Old Ramon moved on forward, reaching out with his stick. Suddenly the snake struck at the tip of the stick flicking near its head and as it stretched out some and before it could recoil Old Ramon lashed down with the stick end just behind its head and it writhed on the ground with a broken neck. Quickly Old Ramon dropped the stick across it, close by the head, and stepped with one boot on the stick to hold it down and with the heel of the other boot stomped the squirming flat head deep into the sandy ground. He pulled from the leather sheath at his waist his knife with the long wicked always razor-edged blade and reached down and cut the rattles from the still twitching tail. He put the knife back in its sheath and picked up the stick and came toward the boy. He held out the rattles on the palm of his hand.

The sheep were silent now, still staring, those in the close-pressed circle, but silent. In the hot stillness the boy stared up at Old Ramon. He was very pale. He dropped his head and looked at the ground. "I do not want it," he said.

Old Ramon held the small cone of rattles between his thumb and forefinger and looked closely at it. "But it is complete," he said. "Even the button-nub is here. It is not often one finds such a fine one. The snakes break them. I do not know how unless it is bumping against stones but they break them."

The boy was silent, staring down by his feet where the black dog crouched, belly to the ground. Old Ramon shrugged his shoulders and tucked the rattles into the remnant of torn pocket of his faded old shirt. He turned away to look out over the flock that was moving restlessly, spreading out,

"There was no need to hit him so hard," said the boy.

"Eh?" said Old Ramon, turning back. "You mean the dog? Ai, it was hard. But it was for his own good. The snake is quicker than the dog. What is it to have a dead snake if you have a dead dog also?"

The boy scuffed with one foot in the sand beside the dog at his feet. "Perhaps that is so. But it was too hard."

"Name of a name!" shouted Old Ramon in exasperation. "Is it that a man must measure out how hard he hits when he must move fast like the snake itself? Was there time to talk to him? No! Was there time to explain to him why he must not act like the fool he tries to be? No! Was there time to think that one will hit this hard or that hard? No! Ten thousand times no! I do not like what there can be in your words! Ramon has done many things in his life that he should not have done! But never in all the years of his life has he hit a dog just for the hitting!"

The sun beat down and the sheep moved restlessly in the hot stillness and Old Ramon stared at the boy standing quiet, very quiet, with head down. He took off his big old hat and wiped around his head and put the hat on at a new angle. He drew in a long breath and let it ease out slowly. "Look now. I will tell him. And if he is the dog that he should be he will know."

Old Ramon squatted on his heels facing the black dog that cringed even lower and would not look at him and inched back farther from him. "Sancho," he said. His voice was low and soft and seemed to come from far back in his throat and the black dog stopped inching back and looked at him. "Ai, Sancho, you who are young and act before you think. It is true that I hit you. But I did not hit you in anger. It was to keep you from the poison. Ramon has lived all the years of his life with the dogs and they are to him like the children he has not had. If he were not a man he would want the good God to make him a dog. Do you think that he would hit you without reason?"

The black dog was inching forward now and the boy watched, fascinated, and Old Ramon's voice went on, low and soft in his throat. "Ai, Sancho. You thought to protect us and the sheep and that was brave. But with the snake, no. That was foolish. The snake is for the man to kill. For the man with the stick that the poison cannot harm. Perhaps it is that you will remember that the next time."

The black dog was close to Old Ramon now and it stretched out its head and licked his hand and Old Ramon rubbed his hand over its head and on the instant of feeling the touch, the reassurance of it, the black dog jumped up and bounded about and jumped in close and brushed against Old Ramon and then to the boy and pushed against him.

The boy stooped to put his arms around the dog's neck and wrestle a bit with him. "I think that he will remember. I think that he has learned."

Old Ramon was upright, looking around at the flock. The sheep were scattered some, moving about. An old brown dog with tongue hanging in the hot glare was racing to close them together and start them again in the right direction. "Pedro did not have to learn," said Old Ramon shortly. He swung away to help the brown dog. The flock, forming again, plodded on.

The boy stood still, watching the flock move. He became aware again of the black dog by his feet. "Sancho. They do not need us. But we must do what we can. Go to the flock." The black dog bounded ahead and stopped and looked back and the boy waved at him to go on. Slowly the boy walked back and took the lead rope of the burro. Slowly he plodded after the flock and Old Ramon striding behind it, urging the stragglers on.

The boy walked slowly in the dust drifting back and then his pace began to quicken and he was jerking on the lead rope and after a while he was beside Old Ramon. They plodded on together in the silence broken only by the occasional coughing and the rustling of the many small hoofs.

"I think," said the boy, "that I would like to have it."

Old Ramon did not look at him but he reached in the remnant of the pocket of his shirt and took out the small cone of rattles. He held it out and the boy took it from him. There were six rings, hard and horny to the feel, and movable to make the whirring noise, dwindling down to the button-nub of the tip.

"The sun today is very strong," said Old Ramon. "It is strong like it was in the Mojave. It makes a man hot in the head so that he says things he could wish he had not said. . . ."

With the lead rope in one hand and the cone of rattles clenched in the other, the boy strode along. His head was high and there was no stare in his eyes. He was thinking that once the father of his father had strode along thus with Old Ramon.

7   THE AIR lay hot and heavy over the big land. The accumulated heat of the whole day seemed to have given it weight to press down on the plodding flock. The sun was low toward the western horizon but there was no lessening of its glare over the dry sands. No breath of a breeze moved. The dust stirred by the many small hoofs clung about the flock and hung motion-

less in the air behind it. Through the dust strode Old Ramon, using his stick much now, urging the stragglers on. Off to one side, out of the dust, plodded the boy, leading the burro. His body slumped some into each plodding step and if he was thinking it was of the wearying seeming endless effort of putting one foot before the other onward.

Old Ramon moved over to the side by the boy, out of the dust. He stopped and the boy stopped too. Old Ramon pulled his hat brim low against the slant light of the sun and looked out all around the far shimmering horizon.

"I have the feeling of it," he said. "Where are the winds of the afternoon that the heat breeds and that bring some coolness to the man and the beast? They are not here. I have the feeling inside, in the bones. They are in hiding. They are building up their strength in their hiding to take us of a suddenness with the surprise."

The boy licked his dry lips. "I do not understand."

"The chorro," said Old Ramon. "The sandstorm." He scanned the horizon again. "Ai, do you see?" Far to the south the horizon was fading.

The land and the sky were merging in the one murky brownness that caught glints from the slant light of the sun and flickered with flashes of color. It was beautiful in the distance but there was darkening menace in it.

Old Ramon stepped to the burro and leaned his weight pressing down on its back. It spread its legs a bit and braced them against the pressure. While the boy watched in wonder Old Ramon climbed on his hand and knees on the burro's back and the two lashed packs that balanced each other on the two sides. The burro braced its legs and they quivered some but it held firm. Carefully Old Ramon steadied himself and rose upright. He peered all around into the distances, studying the land. He jumped down and the burro, released from his weight, shook itself until the packs rattled in the stillness.

Old Ramon whipped a faded bandanna from somewhere out of the recesses of his patched old clothes and handed it to the boy. "Tie this around your mouth and your nose. And tightly." He dropped his stick and took out his knife and pulled at his old shirt until one of the tattered tails was free of his belt and with a single slash he cut this off. In a moment the knife was back in its sheath and the piece of shirt was tied around his head covering his mouth and nose. His voice had a muffled sound under the cloth.

"Follow closely now! You must not lose me and the flock!" He snatched up his stick and ran toward the flock that had moved on. As he ran he pushed up the cloth to get two fingers in his mouth and whistled sharply. "Eh, Pedro! You have the feel also! You have seen! Turn them, my Pedro! Turn them! And hurry!"

The boy, following, saw Old Ramon motioning with wide sweeps of an arm to the west and on around to the northwest, and the old dog, a brown flash in the bright sunlight, driving in along the flock, not gently now, but fiercely, forcing the leaders in an arc toward the west, toward the northwest. The boy's head lifted some as he saw the black dog, seeming to understand, race around to the same side to help.

The flock was stringing out, hurrying, the faster pulling ahead in the lead, a stretched-out curve of trotting, bobbing, spurting sheep flowing over the land. Then Old Ramon was whistling and shouting and waving again and the brown dog was around on the other side, straightening the curve, and the flock flowed, fast for a flock and fleeing, into the northwest. The two dogs raced along the sides, holding the sheep into the long stretched line, and Old Ramon wove from side to side behind with his stick leaping and prodding at the slow ones, the stragglers, and the boy was running, jerking on the lead rope, and slowing to catch his breath and running again.

Suddenly the glare of the sun faded and was gone. High overhead great dust-colored clouds like a curtain had shut it off. The light of the day dimmed in a strange brownish dimness and the first gusts of wind, whirling, raising dust devils, skittered past. The boy ran, holding firmly to the rope, his eyes blinking fast at the dust everywhere in the air now and fixed on the figure of Old Ramon ahead. He could see nothing distinct but he sensed that the ground sloped slightly downwards and then that they had turned some. The sand was looser, thicker under his feet, like the bed of an arroyo.

The wind struck, a wall of rushing air down the slope. Its shrill wail sounded overhead and under this the dull heavy rumbling of the great gusts like a throbbing fast drumbeat. All the land around was blotted out by the flying dust and sand. The boy could stand only by leaning against the wind as if it were something solid and could breathe only by turning his head from it. The sand stung like needles even through his clothes and searched out every place to enter and scratched against his skin. He staggered and stumbled as the gusts beat against him and he could barely make out the blurred figure of Old Ramon ahead and then that faded and he could see nothing. He staggered on and there was nothing. The wind was cold, chilling, shaking after the heat of the sun only a few moments before. He shook and shivered and was battered sideways and he was alone with the burro and the whole wide rest of the world was blotted out and there was only the flying sand and the battering wind. He stumbled to his knees and did not try to get to his feet again. He crouched low, his back to the wind, and buried his head in his arms. He felt the burro jerking on the rope and he clenched his hand tighter on it and crouched even lower to the ground.

The wind shrieked overhead and throbbed its drums and the sand slashed at him. The two of them together, the wind and the sand, seemed to be trying to tear the clothes from his body. His shoulders shook, not alone from the wind and the chill, but from the sobbing effort to breathe.

Faintly he heard a voice. It seemed to come from far away and to go rushing past before he could catch it. It was from behind and to the left. He raised his left arm a bit and peered under it. A blurred shape was coming toward him. It came closer and it was Old Ramon, seeming tall and enormous with the storm whipping around him, striding through it, leaning against the wind. His big old hat was pulled down, clear down over his ears, and with the piece of shirt tied over his mouth and nose all of his face was hidden except the old eyes glinting under thick brows heavy now with sand. He squatted down by the boy. His voice was a muffled shouting snatched by the wind.

"Ai, are you a badger to try to burrow in the ground! It is only a little wind playing its games!"

He took the rope and pulled it until the burro, sidling with rump to the wind, was within reach. "Listen, now. The chorro is nothing to the burro. He has the eyes and the nose and the tough skin for it. You will take hold of the pack ropes on the other side and bend down and go along with him. He will break the wind for you. And it is not far."

Old Ramon rose and pulled the boy up and pushed him around by the side of the burro. He strode off, leaning against the wind, and as the rope tightened the burro swung to follow and the boy, clinging to the ropes, head down, eyes closed, half walking, half dragged, moved along too.

Suddenly the boy was aware that the wind was not so strong. It howled and throbbed overhead, louder, worse than before. But it no longer whipped around and under and over the burro as if trying to get at him, to clutch him, to tear him away. He opened his eyes and raised his head a bit. The air was full of swirling dust and sand but the wind, the great remorseless clutching blast that never stopped and only rose and fell in intensity, could not reach him. It was rushing past overhead. The arroyo had deepened and there were banks more than head-high on each side.

The burro stopped. The boy straightened and looked around. In the weird dim light that was like a dusk only not a dusk he could see some of the sheep. They were huddled together close under one bank and there were others beyond them fading on up the arroyo out of sight in the dusty murk.

"They are all here." Old Ramon was at the other side of the burro, tugging to pull a blanket from under the tight ropes. "Pedro will hold them above. And Sancho. We will stay here below and see that none wander into the wind." He slapped the burro on the rump and it trotted over by the sheep. He put an arm around the boy's shoulders and led him to a hollow in the windward bank where several big boulders and overhang above made a shallow cave. He sat down and pulled the boy down beside him and wrapped the blanket around them both, up and over their heads in back. He pulled the piece of shirt down from his face around his neck and spat to one side. "We are in good time." he said. "I think that now it will really begin to blow."

The boy looked at him, startled, and shrank smaller inside the blanket. His own small hat was down tight over his ears and the bandanna was over his face and his eyes peered out from between, large and staring and blinking much. He listened and the wind was a high thin screeching above and the throbbing under this seemed almost to be shaking the very earth and the dimness increased, strange and unfamiliar, unlike any dimness known before. He shivered and pressed closer to Old Ramon. That was not the wind rushing overhead. It could be many demons shrieking and searching for them.

Old Ramon felt the shivering. "It is only the wind," he said. "It cannot harm us here. I think that it does not even want to harm us. I think that it is glad we have found a safe place. The wind is not angry. The wind is never angry. It is simply big and strong. Most of the time it is gentle and kind. And then once in a long while it remembers its bigness and its strength and is proud and wants to show them. It wants to try to sweep the whole world clean. . . . I think it is talking to us now and the way that the wind talks is to shout. It is saying that it is sorry we picked this day to cross the Jornada Seca because this is the day it has wanted to show its strength."

The boy was silent. He did not seem to hear the words. He still shivered and pressed close. Old Ramon reached up and flipped the blanket from over his head and wrenched his big floppy old hat up off his ears, off his head, and put it back on at a jaunty angle. He pulled the blanket back up over it again. "When you were a small one," he said, "was it that I told you the story of the buffalo bull?"

The boy did not speak. He only shook his head a little.

"This was many years ago," said Old Ramon. "When I was young and could run very fast. One day it was that I saw a round little hill, shaped like a cone, like the crown of my hat. Do you hear me? Do you understand how that hill was shaped?"

The boy pushed up on his own hat to loosen it some and to hear better. He looked sidewise at Old Ramon. "Like your hat."

"Good. That is important. It came into my mind to climb that hill and I did. I sat up there and looked out for a long time and I felt that I was the king of a small mountain. I started down and about half of the way down I saw sleeping on the side of the hill a buffalo bull. He was big. Ah, he was a big one. He was the grandfather of all buffalo bulls."

The boy looked directly at him. "Where was

this? There are no buffalo in this part of the country."

"It was where it was," said Old Ramon. "That is not important. It came into my mind to have the fun with that buffalo. I picked up a big round stone and started it rolling down at him and I hid behind a rock. Bumpity-bump-bump-bump went that stone and bounced and hit that buffalo on the head right between the horns that were so big and long and sharp. He jumped up and snorted and he pawed at the ground and smoke came out of his nostrils and fire came from his mouth —"

"That is silly," said the boy. "The buffalo cannot breathe fire."

"Eh?" said Old Ramon. "And who is telling this story? To whom does this story belong? I say that fire came out of his mouth and smoke and many sparks. It was the big anger burning in him that made the fire. It turned black the grass on the ground in front of him. He sniffed the air and he smelled me and then he saw me. The rock was not big enough to hide all of me. And he came roaring and blowing fire and shaking those big horns toward me up that hill."

Old Ramon stopped and spat to one side. "And then?" said the boy.

"And then I remembered something. The man cannot run as fast as the buffalo. Not up or down a hill. No. But sideways around the sloping of a hill is another thing. Then it is that the great weight of the buffalo keeps pulling him downwards and he runs at a slant and has to keep coming back up again. So I ran around the sloping of that hill and that buffalo could not catch me. Always he kept slanting downwards and had to come up some again. Ah, but he was angry. He galloped and snorted and galloped and blew out fire and soon there was a black ring around that hill from the scorching and there was smoke from his nostrils and from our fast running around it also. The next day I heard from people who saw it from a distance that they thought it was a volcano. And around and around we went and he could not catch me. And then I saw that he was coming closer and closer, that he was not going downwards any more. We were running around that hill to the left always. All that running in that way had made his right legs stretch more and more because of the sloping of the hill until they were longer than his left legs and he could run without slanting on the side of the hill. He was gaining on me and I could feel on my back the heat from the fire from his mouth. . . ."

Old Ramon lifted the piece of shirt that was around his neck up to his nose and blew into it vigorously.

"Why do you stop?" said the boy. "What did you do then?"

"It was simple," said Old Ramon. "I turned and ran down the hill and out on the level ground. And the buffalo could not run straight down after me. His right legs were longer and when he tried to run straight he kept going in circles to the left. He tried and he tried and he kept going in circles until he was dizzy and fell down in a daze."

The boy was not shivering. He was sitting up straighter inside the blanket. "I do not believe that story," he said. "Not one word of it."

"Eh?" said Old Ramon. "And did anyone here ask that you believe it? . . . But if you will look out you will see that the chorro is passing."

The light was stronger in the arroyo now, the dust and sand filtering down out of the air. The wind no longer rushed in great blasts overhead with the shrieks of demons. It sang softly in long sweeps and was the familiar wind of the evenings after the heat of the days. The sheep were stirring, moving apart some and shaking themselves.

"Ai," said Old Ramon. "They will not want to hurry much for a while. They are heavy with the sand in their wool. But it will work out as they move." He pushed up and went to a sloping place along the bank and scrambled to the top. He stood tall looking up the arroyo and whistled and waved. From on up the arroyo the sheep began to move, to crowd down toward those nearby and these too began to move, down the arroyo toward the open again. Old Ramon stood on the bank and watched them. The last of the flock moved by below him with the brown dog urging them on and he came scrambling down the bank.

"There are three missing," he said. "And where is that Sancho?"

There was a barking up the arroyo and then three sheep came trotting heavily and behind them the black dog, bounding and nipping at them. The boy saw and jumped up and hurried to Old Ramon, trailing the blanket. "Do you see?"

"I see," said Old Ramon. "I think it is that Pedro sent him after them. And he has them. He has done well."

Old Ramon took the blanket and shook it and began to fold it and stow it under the pack ropes again.

"But how could you count them?" said the boy. "So many and all moving."

"Eh, that?" said Old Ramon. "There is a trick to that also. Each pastor has his own way. I do it by the fives. I see the sheep by the fives at the time and I keep count of the fives on my fingers. When all the fingers are used once, that is the fifty. Twice, it is the hundred. My cousin Pablo who thinks he is so clever uses the threes. He can keep track of the threes well enough. But then he has to scratch his hard head and figure a while what that many threes mean. But come. We have lost time and we still have far to go. . . ."

The flock had formed out on the level and plodded on. Far to the north the trailing dust clouds showed against the horizon but here now the soft wind was cool and the air was fresh and sweet and the light of the setting sun was a splendor up the western sky. "Ah," said Old Ramon, drawing in a deep breath of the sweet cool air. "The chorro has swept the world clean again."

The flock plodded on and the boy strode beside Old Ramon and the burro followed.

"When you are in the school again," said Old Ramon, "you can say to the other boys that you have been in a storm of storms."

The boy looked sideways up at him. "So it was bad then?"

"Yes," said Old Ramon. "It was bad. It did not last long. But it was very bad. And now it is that we have several hours yet to journey. Are you tired?"

"I am tired," said the boy. "But that is a nothing. There is a new strength in my legs."

The flock plodded on and the two dogs trotted out at the sides and the sun dropped below the mountains and the swift dusk of the high country swept over the big land.

"It will be dark soon," said Old Ramon. "And no moon. You will not be afraid?"

"I will not be afraid," said the boy. "You are here."

The flock plodded on into the approaching night, a grayish shifting shape flowing over the darkening land.

"Ramon," said the boy. "I do not understand about that story. When the buffalo ran around the hill his right legs stretched longer. Why did not your right leg stretch longer also?"

"Eh?" said Old Ramon. "So you think to catch Ramon in that way? I will tell you. That is simple also. I ran frontwards until my right leg stretched a little and then I turned with my face to the buffalo and ran backwards until my left leg stretched to match and thus it was that I kept them even. . . ."

8   THE HILLS rose dark and rounded
in the night toward the far heights of the mountains beyond. At their edging where a smattering
of grass began and a small spring fed a small pool
the flock was bedded. The last embers of the little
fire nearby made a tiny pinpoint of living spark
in the immensity of the big land. Old Ramon
sat close, wrapped in his blanket, and watched the

glowing of the embers fade. A few feet away the boy lay on the ground, a shapeless roll in his blanket.

The boy stirred and he too sat up, holding the blanket about him. "It is very late," he said. "And yet I cannot sleep. How is that?"

"It is often so after a long day and into the night," said Old Ramon. "The man then is too tired to sleep right away. His head is full of the long journeying and his muscles are tight. He must sit quiet and let the tightness slip away and then between a word and a wink of the eye the sleep creeps on him."

Slow moments moved and from beyond the flock came a long low howling that seemed a part of the dark vastness around, that climbed in tone and intensity and broke off in a series of short yappings. The boy sat up straighter and looked around toward the packs and the loaded rifle leaning against one of them.

"There is no need of the gun," said Old Ramon. "It is only the coyote. I think that he is saying things about us and our using his water hole. I do not think they are nice things. But he will not harm the flock. Pedro is there."

The howling came again, long and long-drawn. It died away and was followed by barking from close by the flock, barking angry and challenging.

"That is Sancho," said Old Ramon. "He is young. He talks back. But it is useless. That is what the coyote wants, to insult the dogs and make them angry. That is his game now. He would make no noise if he thought that he could get a one of the sheep. I think that already he has tried and that now he knows. Pedro is there."

The howling came again and broke into many short barks and yappings. It was several sounds at once seeming to come from several places.

The boy sat up straight again. "There are more of them!"

Old Ramon chuckled, a reassuring sound in the night. "There is only the one. Ah, he is smart, Don Coyote. That is one of his little tricks. To throw his voice and sound like many. I think there are as many stories about him as there are hairs in his own tail. When we are settled on in the hills for a time I will tell some of them to you. . . . Ai, he is a nuisance and a thief and an insulter of good dogs. But he is Don Coyote. Ramon would miss him if he were gone, if his kind were all killed. He is like a voice of the land and of the night over the land. . . . Ai, ai, he is smart. He is not big but he is very clever. I have known him to sneak to a flock in the bright light of the day and pick a sheep too stupid to know he is not a dog and take hold of her wool and pull and lead her away far enough so that the noise of her killing would not be heard. And that with a lazy dog asleep close by. . . . And he knows the gun, even the pistol that is small and carried at the belt. A man walks with a gun and the coyote sees him but he never sees the coyote. He walks without a gun and Don Coyote may not move much more than to get out of the way unless a dog is there to chase him. Ai, he is cunning and full of tricks. But my Pedro knows them all. . . ."

The howling came again, farther away and fading, and then there was only the soft cool silence of the night. The boy shifted a little in his blanket. "Ramon. Is it not sometimes lonely, tending the sheep?"

"I suppose it is so for some men," said Old Ramon slowly. "For those who are accustomed to the towns and the clutter and the clatter of many people about. It has never been so for Ramon. It is never so for the true herder of sheep, for the man with the feel of the flock born in him. . . . I have thought much about that. I think that it rests upon what a man is in himself, on the inside of him. I think that to be alone is one thing and that to be lonely is another thing altogether. I have felt the loneliness when I was in a town with many people around me. I think that is because it was a strange town to me and I did not know the people. But I have never felt the loneliness when I was alone with my flock even in the far valleys of the mountains and no other people within many miles. I think perhaps that is because I know this land and its people that are the wild things living in it and nothing of it is strange to me. . . . I do not see how a man can be lonely when the good God's world is open around him, when there is the sun that shines by day and the stars that look down by night and the wind that blows and the mountains that watch all and everything and the grass that grows, when there are the sheep that need him to care for them and the dogs to help him and Don Coyote to call him names and the owl to ask him questions from hidden places. . . ."

"I think," said the boy, "that my father is right. There are many things that are not in the books." He lay back down and put his arms up, elbows out, his hands clasped like a pillow under his head. "And I am wondering, Ramon. Have you always tended the sheep?"

"Not always," said Old Ramon. "There was a time, no. And that was a bad time."

"Tell me," said the boy.

"Your father is not right on all things," said Old Ramon. "I have lost lambs. . . . " He stared into the small heap of ashes that had been the last embers and was silent.

"You are my book," said the boy. "Can you not tell me?"

"It was the wine," said Old Ramon. "Ai, the wine. . . . When the money was gone and I came back from the California, your grandfather had many sheep. I worked for him. I worked well, yes. Always the knowing of the sheep has been in me. We had been young together and held each other up in the days of hot sun and no water and the fierce chorro of the Mojave. And now he was my patrón and I was only one of his pastores and that was right. He was much man. And I worked well. You must remember that. But when I was paid and there was money in my pocket, I could not work. I must spend it. And when the money was gone I would go to him again. Always he would say the same thing. 'Ramon,' he would say. 'As long as I have sheep, you have a flock.' And thus it was for some years. And one time in the lambing season, it was before we would go out with the flocks, I was to watch for the night in the big corral, and my cousin Pablo came by and he had two bottles of wine he was taking to his house. I made him leave a one of them with me. Ai, there is no need to tell what happened. You should know how the ewes are with the lambs. There are those who will not know their own lambs when they are first born and the man must make them to nurse for the first time so that they know them. There are those who have the twins, the two at once, and perhaps they will claim only the one and the man must make them take the other. And those with the new lambs must be kept separate from the others so that the little new ones with their wobbly legs are not trampled if there is a scaring and the sheep push about and crowd together. . . .

"Ai, it was that I lay like a piece of the dead

wood with the wine in me and in the early morning when I woke with a head very heavy there were seven dead lambs. I was ashamed. I could not have looked the father of your father in the face that day. I told myself that I had lived so long with the sheep that I was become stupid like them. I hurried away and I went far away and I did not come back. I went to this place and to that place and I worked for many men and I did many things. Ah, yes, Ramon could do much in those days. He could ride the horse and herd the cattle. He could drive the mules with the big freight wagons. He could work all the day in the hot sun without tiring building the adobe walls. He could drink the wine and fight with the other men and use the knife like the lion of the mountains his claws. But he could not think about himself without the shame. Always he remembered those seven lambs. . . . and the running away from the face of his friend. . . ."

Old Ramon stared into the small heap of ashes and was silent.

"And then?" said the boy softly.

"And then one day I was working with others on a road that was for the stagecoaches. And I heard it. I heard the blethering of a flock that was passing by. I saw the sheep moving and I saw the pastor and his dog and I smelled the smell of the sheep and of the good dust drifting in the air from their hoofs. I had a shovel in my hands. I laid that shovel on the ground and I walked away. Four days I walked and I came to the hacienda of your grandfather. There was much happening around the buildings and the corrals. They were preparing flocks to go into the hills. And there was a man in charge giving orders whom I had never seen before. He told me that my patrón, the father of your father, had fallen from a horse two months before and the horse had rolled on him and three days later he died. . . . Ai . . . ai . . . I stood there in my sorrow and remembering my shame, and that man became angry at me. He told me to go away and that he had no place there for me. And I saw coming from the house a young man, still very young and not much more yet than a boy, but slim and straight like your grandfather. It was four years and more but I knew him. And he knew me. He put an arm around me and he stood slim and straight beside me and he said to that man: 'This is the Ramon who took my father across the Mojave when there were no trails and in the year of the great dryness.' And the man said: 'And what is that? I have heard of him. He drinks too much of the wine and he is too free with his knife and he loses the lambs.' And the young man who is now your father spoke proudly like the true patrón he would be. 'That is enough of such talk,' he said. 'What are the lambs? A nothing. There is a writing in our house that my father left. It says that as long as my family has sheep, Ramon has a flock.'

"Ai," said Old Ramon. "Your father is a man of much business now. He passes most of his time in the town. But he also is much man. And what can Ramon do for a patrón like that? He can lose no more lambs and bring in his flock fat and well fleeced. And he can remember. . . ."

9   THE BURRO chewed steadily on a mouthful of good grass from beside the limp lead rope on the ground and waited patiently for the packs to be removed. A few feet away Old Ramon leaned on his stick with one hand and shaded his eyes with the other against the red-gold light of the setting sun. At his feet lay the brown dog. Together the man and the dog looked out over the

wide green hollow in the hills where the flock watered at a small stream and the boy and the black dog stood close by.

The last sheep finished their watering and turned away to join the rest of the flock. The boy motioned in a sweeping gesture with one arm and the black dog bounded forward and caught itself and slowed and went around to one side of the flock and the boy moved to the other. Working together, on their opposite sides, the boy and the dog pushed at the flock, gently, gently, and it drifted away from the water and it closed more compactly and the boy and the dog moved ahead of it and stopped it, and the boy moved back and forth holding it while the dog circled, closing in stragglers. Here and there sheep folded their front legs under and lay down and then more and more of them and at last all but five were bedded down and these stood stubborn and upright in their scattered spots. The boy put his hands on his hips and stared at these five, one after the other, and shook his head in irritation.

Old Ramon put two fingers in his mouth and whistled. The boy looked toward him. Old

Ramon beckoned the boy to come. The boy started toward him and broke into a run and the black dog bounded after him and ahead of him and all around him and the boy tripped over the dog and the two rolled over and wrestled on the ground with laughter and barking mingled and got to their feet and came to Ramon and the brown dog and the burro.

"It is easy," said the boy. "One pushes, gently, gently, and soon the stupid sheep think they want what one desires them to want. But those silliest of all the silly ones. They will not lie down."

"No." said Old Ramon. "Always when a flock is bedded there are those that stand and watch. They watch for their period and then they lie down and others stand. I have heard it said that this is perhaps a memory from the times before men and dogs watched for them. But that there ever were such times I do not know. And it is stupid because they have forgotten, if indeed they ever knew, what to do if danger does come. But you would have known that some would stand if you had watched more closely on the yesterdays before today."

The boy looked quickly away and then down at the black dog by his feet and bent to scratch the dog's head.

"That Sancho is learning," said Old Ramon.

The boy looked up quickly. "Do you think that some day he will be as good as Pedro?"

Old Ramon leaned on his stick. "Can a man say with certainty what tomorrow will bring? I have had many dogs and each one I hold in my mind for this thing and for that thing which was good. But in all the years of my life there has been one Pedro. I have told you of his great-grandfather who took the flock to water across the Mojave. Pedro is like him. But he is more. He is my Pedro. Watch now and he will show you a small something." Old Ramon looked down at the old brown dog. "Pedro. It has seemed to me in today's journeying that perhaps Maria walked with a limp. Maria. Bring her to me."

The brown dog rose and trotted toward the flock and along it searching for the right ewe and wove his way and nipped her protesting to her feet and forced her out into the open. Once in the open she dodged in spurts to get back and the brown dog leaped in flashes of speed to head her and drove her swinging around toward Old Ramon.

"Now hold her," said Old Ramon.

The brown dog leaped in close and gripped the heavy wool of her neck in his jaws and braced himself, holding. Old Ramon dropped his stick and stepped forward and ran his hands over the ewe. One hand strayed briefly and ruffled through the shaggy fur of the brown dog's head and neck. "Eh, Pedro? You could have told me, eh? It is that I was wrong. She is sound as a church bell. Good. Now take her back."

The brown dog released the ewe and nipped at her heels and she ran, indignant and protesting, for the safety of the flock, and the dog trotted after.

Old Ramon picked up his stick. "There is little light left. We must hurry to make camp. We will use the little tent because we shall stay in this valley for some days. . . ."

10   Old Ramon and the boy slept
well in the wide low little tent that was not much
higher than a man's head when he sat up. It
was darker inside than in the night outside where
the soft rounded land rising to the mountains
beyond glowed faintly under the thin light of the
new moon that hung ready to drop behind a high
hill to the west.

Abruptly the boy struggled up out of sleep. A deep-toned barking sounded outside, coming closer. He sensed Old Ramon scrambling past him in the darkness, out of the tent. He scrambled after and in the dimness outside saw Old Ramon stretching up tall and the brown dog bounding in, no longer barking, with a deep rumbling in its throat.

"What is it?" cried the boy.

"The wolf!" said Old Ramon. "Pedro says the wolf!"

The boy crouched by the tent opening and saw Old Ramon take the old single-shot rifle from its place by the packs and start away and the brown dog streak into the night ahead of him.

Old Ramon paused and looked back. "You will stay here. You will build up the fire and then bring me a torch." And Old Ramon was a dark shape in the night running after the brown dog.

The boy shook himself to stop the shivering and began to put wood from the ready pile on the remains of the fire. He knelt to blow on the sparks that stirred in the ashes. Out in the night the old gun roared once and a silence followed and then the voice of Old Ramon struck through the silence. "Pedro! The flock! The flock!"

Tiny flames began to lick up through the fresh wood and the boy stood and peered into the night. The flock was a compact grayish blotch out in the hollow. All the sheep were on their feet, drawn together, close packed, and two dark shapes ran toward them, an old man and an old dog. The man strode in among them, bending down to force them aside with great heaves of his arms and shoulders, and the dog leaped up on the close-packed backs and ran on these in toward the center of the flock.

The boy watched in dazed wonder and suddenly remembered. He looked about and took a piece of piñon, knotted at one end, and laid this end in the growing fire. It caught and flames fed on the pitch of the knotted end and he took hold of the other end and ran toward the flock, holding the piece up as a torch.

The sheep were scattered some now, spread out in bunches with spaces between. The brown dog circled wide, watching that none should break away into the night. Old Ramon stood by the outer rim of the flock, reaching for breath in long slow gaspings. The boy stared at him in the flickering light of the torch.

"But — but — I do not understand," said the boy.

"There is no other animal — not even the chicken — so stupid as the sheep. . . . Danger comes in the night — perhaps they run — at once and all together — here and there and everywhere — that is bad — a whole day and more to gather them. . . . Perhaps they do not run — they press together as tonight — they huddle in one tight mass — that is worse — in the middle they are squeezed — the smaller ones go down and others cover them — they cannot breathe — and some die. . . ."

Old Ramon took the torch and strode away and the boy followed. Old Ramon stooped and picked the old gun from the ground and strode on. He bent down, holding the torch low to light the ground, and moved slowly, searching. He stopped and bent lower and peered at the ground by his feet. "Do you see? The tracks. Big, very big. And here is blood. Ah, that wolf is hit. He will not be back. This time of the year he should be in the mountains, in the big timber. He will hurry there now."

Old Ramon moved slowly again, searching over the ground. "Good. Good. There was but one. That is very good." He straightened and looked all around and seemed to be listening. He shook his head and looked at the boy and started to speak and then did not and looked away and moved again, swinging back toward the far side of the flock. He moved back and forth, watching the ground. He stopped again and the boy moved up beside him. Together they looked down at the black still shape on the ground, at the muzzle stretched out with the lips drawn back from the teeth, at the flickering light of the torch reflected from the staring sightless eyes and from the splotch of dark blood by the torn throat.

"Ai, the fool," said Old Ramon softly. "Ai, the brave young foolish one."

The boy's breath caught in a sob. "Let the tears come," said Old Ramon softly. "They are good for you. And the dog will know. The spirit of the dog will know. . . . You will wait here with him and no one will see. And in a while I will

come with the little shovel. We will bury him
deep. And stones from the stream bed will mark
the spot. . . .

11 THE FIRE fought back the now moonless dark with its small wavering circle of light. Old Ramon sat close to it, his legs hunched up and his arms wrapped around them, his chin sunk on his knees. He stared into the small flickering flames. Part way around the fire to his left sat the boy, cross-legged, his body slumped forward with his elbows on his knees, and he too stared into the flames.

"It is always so," said Old Ramon. "There is no sleep for the master on the night that a dog dies."

Slow moments moved and a dim shape slipped silently up to the opposite outer edge of the firelight.

"Yes," said Old Ramon. "Yes, Pedro. It is that you may be with us for a while."

The old brown dog came forward, on its way to Old Ramon's side, and stopped by the boy to nuzzle gently against him.

"Ai," said Old Ramon. "Pedro knows."

Suddenly the boy pushed at the old dog and struck out at him. "Coward! Get away from me.!"

The brown dog moved over by Old Ramon and lay down beside him and Old Ramon straightened some and looked at the boy. "And how is that?"

"He came running to us and left Sancho to fight the wolf!"

Old Ramon stared into the flames again. "Yes. That is what he did. And because he did that we have lost no sheep. . . . To be brave is a fine thing.

But it is not enough. One must be wise too. And Pedro knows. . . . What you must know is that the good sheep dog thinks always of the flock. The dogs are no match for the wolf. For the coyote, yes. For the big wolf of the timber, no. The wolf is bigger, faster, more fierce. In him is the strength of the wild life. He has jaws that are like a great trap and teeth that can slice deep like this knife that I carry. I have seen one wolf kill three good dogs in little more time than it takes to say the words. And so it is that when the wolf comes, the good sheep dog runs to waken the man and his gun. And so it is that then the flock may be safe and what is needful may be done. And Pedro knows. . . . "

"I don't care!" The boy's voice broke and he looked away. "It is the knowing of a coward! To be safe! To run away!" The boy's head dropped forward and sank between his arms and his knees.

Old Ramon stared into the fire. He spoke softly. "Pedro. My Pedrocito. There is one here who thinks that you think to be safe. To run from the danger. Go to him and let him feel of your side." And the brown dog rose and moved over by the boy and Old Ramon spoke again, sharply. "Put out your hand. Feel there along his side, under the fur."

Slowly the boy straightened some and reached with one hand and touched the dog. Slowly his fingers worked down through the shaggy fur and felt the long hardened furrows of scar tissue on the skin. He straightened more and pulled his hand back and the old brown dog sank down to lie beside him.

"A wolf?" said the boy.

"No," said Old Ramon. "Not the wolf. The bear. The great grizzly bear."

The boy sat very straight. "Tell me."

"I will tell you. You were small and away with your mother in the town. It was six years ago. It was perhaps seven years. I would have to figure back and that is no matter. We had been, I say Pedro and I, to see my cousin Pablo and his daughter's wedding. We were coming back and over the mountains because that way was the shorter. I walked and carried the gun and Pedro followed and we walked fast because my patrón, your father, waited for us with many sheep. It was a high trail and very rough and through many big rocks. Of a suddenness, I do not know just how, around a twist of the trail among the rocks, and he was there, the bear, not twenty feet in front of me. He was so startled that he thought only to fight, to kill, and he growled horribly and showed his big teeth and came toward me. And I, I, Ramon, who am an old man enough and have seen enough to know about such things, I was so startled too that I stepped back and I tripped and fell and the gun flew out of my hand. . . . "

Old Ramon paused and looked at the brown dog. The dog's head was up, pointed toward him, and a low rumbling sounded in its throat. "Do you see? He knows I am telling about him. And about the bear. And he remembers."

The boy too looked at the dog. "And what then?"

"That is how it was. I was down and the gun was many feet away and the bear was close upon me. And from the trail behind me like a whirl of the wind, like a mad bull in the charge, came my Pedro. Every hair on him stood out stiff like a brush and he too growled horribly and he leaped straight at the bear. While I scrambled on my hands and my knees and scratched myself on the stones after the gun, I saw Pedro with his teeth tight in the bear's neck and the bear rearing up on his hind legs and thrashing his head and making Pedro bounce and snap like a whip in the air and then one big paw with its great claws came slashing down along Pedro's side and ripped him loose and threw him many feet away. But it was enough. I had the gun. I shot well. I did not have to use my knife. And when I ran to Pedro he could not stand. Some of his entrails hung through the rips in his side. But he still growled and his jaws snapped and he tried to pull himself along the ground toward the bear. And as I looked at him, his eyes closed and he was still. . . ."

Gently the boy reached and felt again through the shaggy fur along the dog's side. "And then?"

"And then I took care of him the best that I could. I used my shirt for the bandage. I tied a cord on the gun and hung it on my back and I carried him. I ran and I walked fast and I ran and old man that I am I cried my tears on the way and when I reached the sheep camp I fell and knew nothing. And when I was myself again I found that my patrón, your father, had brought a doctor and he said that Pedro would live. And Pedro lived. . . ."

Old Ramon stared into the little fire and the boy sat straight with one hand on the old brown dog and he too stared into the fire. Slow moments moved and the boy spoke. "Do you think that perhaps Sancho knew that Pedro would wake us and that is why he stayed to fight the wolf?"

Old Ramon turned his head and looked at the boy a long moment. "It could be," he said slowly. "Yes. It could be. . . ." He roused himself a bit. "Pedro. It is time." And the brown dog rose and trotted off into the night.

The fire dwindled and the man and the boy stared into the embers. "Yes," said the boy. "I think that is right. I think that Pedro was Sancho's book and Sancho watched and listened and Sancho was —"

"Will you be quiet!" Old Ramon thumped a fist on the dry ground beside him. "Ramon is thinking. He is thinking of what he knows of the country to the south of this place. . . ."

The fire dwindled more and Old Ramon sat up straighter. "Yes," he said. "Yes. It can be done. And without harm to the sheep. We will start through the notch at the upper end of this valley when the sun rises. There is water for each day's journey and good grass along the way. We will go slowly so that the sheep can feed well. And on the fifth day we will be in the valley of the white cliffs where my cousin Vincente has a small farm. It is two years ago that we bred his bitch Cloe to my Pedro. It may be that Pedro will have no more breeding because he is old like his master. But I have been told that it is a fine litter. I have been told there is one of them that is like Pedro when he was young. And it is that I have the choice of them in payment for the breeding. . . ."

The boy sat up very straight and looked at Old Ramon, waiting.

"Yes," said Old Ramon. "Yes. For the son of my patrón, the son of my dog. There is a rightness to it."

"Oh . . . Ramon. . ." The boy did not try to say more and, like Old Ramon, he too stared into the embers. Then his head turned. "Does he have a name?"

"A name?" said Old Ramon. "And how should I know that? My cousin Vincente must call him something. But that is a nothing. A dog does not have a real name until he who will be his master gives it to him. But if I were a boy sitting by what remains of this fire, I would know what name I would give. . . ."

Slow moments moved and the man and the boy stared into the last glowing embers.

"Yes," said the boy. "I know. I think that I will call him Sancho."